T H E hoaX F I L E S

this Book Belongs
to:
Alexis Oull

Alexis O

THE HOAX FILES

AN UNAUTHORIZED PARODY
by Alfredo di Darco

ALADDIN PAPERBACKS

First Aladdin Paperbacks edition June 1998

Aladdin Paperbacks
An imprint of Simon & Schuster
Children's Publishing Division
1230 Avenue of the Americas
New York, NY 10020

Designed by Steve Scott
The text for this book was set in Giovanni Book.
Printed and bound in the United States of America
10 9 8 7 6 5 4 3 2 1

Library of Congress Cataloging-in-Publication Data
Di Darco, Alfredo.
The hoaX-FILES : the spoof is out there / by Alfredo di Darco.
p.   cm.
"An unauthorized parody."
Summary: In this parody of the television show and movie,
the X-Files, Agents Moldy and Scolder investigate
three hoaX-Files, #1: Alien dogduction,
#2: Ixnay on the eezechay, and #3: Epidermis enigmata.
ISBN 0-689-82185-9 (pbk.)
[1. Extraterrestrial beings—Fiction. 2. Human-alien encoun-
ters—Fiction. 3. Humorous stories.] I. Title.
PZ7.D595Ho   1998
[Fic]—dc21   98-13142
CIP   AC

To my father,
an enthusiastic teller
of bad jokes

TABLE OF CONTENTS

T H E Hoax ⬦ F I L E S

#1: Alien Dogduction

Special FBI Agent Wolf Moldy tossed and turned. Sweat soaked his sheets. He was having The Dream again. It was horrible.

In his dream he was running down the hallway of his house. He was dressed in pajamas—the ones with the little UFOs on them—and he was chasing something—or someone.

A light was shining, brighter than any Earthly light, as if a thousand suns were blazing in Moldy's eyes. The light blinded and confused him. Not only that, it made him wish he'd remembered to wear his sunglasses. And as he ran he heard a noise that filled him with dread. It was barking—the frightened barking of his little dog, Sam.

"Sam! Sam!" Moldy cried in the dream. "Don't worry! I'm coming!" In answer there was a pitiful yowl—as if Sam knew that his master could never run fast enough to catch up to him.

The dream always ended the same way: Moldy reached the end of the hallway, his heart pounding. As he called out to his dog over and over again, the blazing light faded, leaving him in darkness. And Sam—his beloved miniature schnauzer—was gone.

Moldy woke. He sat bolt upright and peered into the corner of the room, feeling sick at heart. Sam's lumpy flannel bed was there, just as it always had been. It still smelled, too—Sam had a powerful scent for such a little dog. But the bed was empty. It had been empty for years, ever since that fateful night when They had come—and taken Sam away.

Why had aliens taken his dog? Why?

Why? Why? The question tormented Wolf Moldy. He knew he couldn't rest until he'd answered it.

"Sam," the troubled agent whispered, "I'll find you, I promise. If it takes me the rest of my—" The phone rang, interrupting his vow, and he picked up.

"Moldy," he snapped. There were only two people who would dare to call him this early in the morning: his partner, Special Agent Doona Scolder, and his personal psychic, Claire Voyance.

It was Scolder. "Moldy," she said, "I just got an urgent call from headquarters. They want to see us right away. Can you meet me there in eighteen seconds?"

"Is a pig's tail pork?" he retorted, hanging up, throwing on his suit and tie, leaping into his car, and taking off.

He made it in seventeen.

There was no telling what kind of mood their boss would be in: bad or very bad. FBI Assistant Director Wally Skunker never smiled. He never joked around. His range of emotions went from gruff to pissed off, with a little smoldering unfriendliness in between. But Moldy and Scolder respected him. He was tough. He was honest. He always gave it to them straight.

This morning was no exception. "Molder, Scoldy," he said, "I'm going to give it to you straight. You look terrible. Scoldy, I hate that dress. Where'd you get it, the town dump? And Molder, that tie sucks. Smiley faces? Give me a break! Furthermore, there's something going on in Cleveland that's stumping the Bureau. A case involving kids—ninth graders. Might be a Hoax File."

"Sounds intriguing," said Moldy, betraying no emotion. Didn't Skunker know that the smiley faces tie was his favorite? And if

Skunker was so brilliant, why couldn't he ever get their names right?

"What's the crime, sir?" asked Scolder. "I mean, besides my dress. Have the kids been killed? Kidnapped? Sold into slavery?"

Skunker frowned and shook his head. "It's worse than that."

Moldy and Scolder waited.

Skunker got up and started pacing the room. "Have either of you heard of someone called Banana Fana Fo-Fana?" he asked gravely.

The agents thought for a moment, then shook their heads.

"That's what I was afraid of," said Skunker. He sat down heavily and stared off into space.

Again, Moldy and Scolder waited. Finally Scolder broke the silence. "Is Banana Fana Fo-Fana an element in this Cleveland case?" she asked.

"What? No. No, it's just a name that's been

rattling around in my head. You know how it is—like a jingle that lodges in your brain. It's been driving me nuts," said Skunker.

The agents looked at each other. Their boss was getting more and more unpredictable these days. Scolder thought it might be the pressure of his job. Moldy suspected something more sinister, like a secret government plot to make Skunker lose his hair. He was already pretty bald.

"Sir?" said Scolder gently. "The Cleveland case? Do you want to tell us some more about it?"

"What? Oh, sure," said Skunker. "Where was I?"

"Kids, sir," said Moldy.

"Oh, that's right." Skunker snapped his fingers, remembering. "Strange outbreak affecting kids—ninth graders. Whole clusters of them acting weird. Not washing their faces. Disobeying their parents. Refusing to do their homework."

"Why is that unusual, sir?" asked Moldy. "Sounds like normal adolescent behavior to me."

"That may be, except for one thing," said Skunker.

"What's that?" asked Moldy.

"They're barking."

"Barking, sir?" said Scolder.

"High-pitched little yips," said Skunker. "Mixed in with their speech. It's bizarre. Listen to this transcript." He read from a report on his desk: "'No, I won't take the garbage out, you dumb WOOF! WOOF!'"

Skunker shook his head, clearly puzzled. He read some more: "'Practice the piano? WOOF, no, you YIP! YIP! YIP!'"

The agents waited. Skunker went on. "It gets worse," he said. "Listen to this: 'No I'm not going to sleep! I don't care if it's past my bedtime! WOOF you and the bike you rode in on!'"

Skunker took off his glasses and rubbed

his eyes as if he were in pain. "Molder, Scoldy," he said. "I'll give it to you straight. You're the only agents I know who can make any sense of this. I want you to get on it right away."

"That's 'Moldy, Scolder,'" corrected Scolder.

"Whatever," snapped Skunker. "Just see what you can find out."

"We'll be on the next plane to Cleveland, sir," said Scolder.

"Smiley tie and all," added Moldy.

Their first stop in Cleveland was the Rock and Roll Hall of Fame.

"This was a good idea, Moldy," Scolder said to her partner as they walked in. "There should be lots of teenagers around. Maybe they'll give us some clues."

"Clues? I didn't come here for clues, Scolder," said Moldy. "I came here to see the

10

exhibits. I've been dying to check out this place. Look!" he cried, pointing to a glass case. "Bo Diddley's guitar! And over there—Keith Moon's drum set! And—oh, my God, this is incredible! Tina Turner's wig!"

Scolder smiled. Her partner's enthusiasm was infectious. Soon she was following him from exhibit to exhibit, enjoying the rock-and-roll memorabilia right along with him. And then it happened—right in front of Jerry Lee Lewis's "Great Balls of Fire" boxer shorts. Moldy froze, turning pale.

Scolder was puzzled. The shorts were outstanding, true. But Moldy's reaction was pretty extreme.

It wasn't the shorts Moldy was reacting to, however. It was the sight of a little gray animal that was scurrying out of the exhibit hall. "Sam?" he gasped, blinking incredulously. "Is that you?" He set off after the animal at a run. Scolder took one last look at the shorts and then ran after her partner.

Had he really seen his long-lost little dog? Or was this another false alarm, like the time he'd chased the squirrel?

It was so sad, Scolder thought as she trailed Moldy through the Hall of Fame. Every time her partner saw a little gray animal, he thought it was his dog, Sam. He'd go off on a wild-goose chase, a chase that always ended the same way: The animal wouldn't be Sam. Sometimes it wouldn't even be a dog. And Moldy would be heartbroken.

She found him at the front entrance. The gray dog was nowhere in sight. "Are you all right, Moldy?" she asked.

He nodded, but there were tears in his eyes. "It—it disappeared before I could catch it," he said haltingly. "I—I could have sworn it was Sam—" he stopped, overcome. Scolder looked at him with pity. Of course she didn't believe that Sam had been taken by aliens. That was just another one of

Moldy's strange paranoid fantasies. But she still felt really sorry that he'd lost his pet. *I wish Sam would come back*, she thought, closing her eyes and crossing her fingers.

It was a wish she would soon regret.

Not far from the Rock and Roll Hall of Fame, a small gray schnauzer with oddly vacant eyes licked itself slowly. The fleas it was carrying sent the dog's brain a message in a language never before heard in this galaxy. Roughly translated, the message was this: Take us to the mall so we can bite more teenagers! The dog, an unwilling victim of the tiny alien creatures, listened. And prepared to obey.

"Now where?" asked Scolder as the two agents walked to their car.

"Where can we find some ninth graders?" asked Moldy.

13

Scolder checked her watch. "It's three-thirty. School's out. I'd say the mall."

"Ordinarily I'd say that was a disappointingly logical solution to a question with such far-reaching implications that only a brilliant, unusual mind like mine could truly answer it," said Moldy.

Scolder looked at her partner. Was she thinking he was a pompous jerk? Nobody would ever know from her expression.

"On the other hand, you may be right," said Moldy. There were moments when he suspected Scolder was just a little bit in love with him—it was this way she had of looking at him sometimes.

"Only one way to find out," said Scolder, climbing into the driver's seat. "Let's go."

When they got to the mall they decided to check out the video arcade first. Which is where they found out that Scolder was right: The place was crawling with kids.

"Let's start questioning them," Moldy

shouted over the electronic din. The loud trills, pings, boings, and screeches—mutant warriors in combat, space vehicles crashing and exploding—made it hard for the two agents to hear each other. Scolder nodded, and they approached a cluster of boys intent on a game of NUKEM.

"Excuse me," said Moldy to one of the boys. "Mind if I ask you a few questions?"

"What about?" sneered the boy. He looked about thirteen years old. His face was filthy—as if he hadn't washed it in weeks.

"Are you in the ninth grade?" asked Moldy.

"Duh, yeah," said the boy. "What's it to you?"

"Did you do your homework last night?" asked Moldy.

"Huh? No!"

"Are you going to do it tonight?"

"No!" Still sneering at Moldy, the boy scratched at his arms as if they were itching.

Moldy shot Scolder a significant look. "What if . . . what if your parents tell you that you have to?" he asked.

"Duh. I won't listen to them," said the boy.

"Me neither," said one of his friends, scratching his neck. His face was really dirty, too.

"WOOF!" exclaimed another boy, scratching at his chest. "Homework sucks."

"YIP! YIP! YIP! It sucks big time!" said the first boy.

The agents looked at each other. They stepped away from the boys. "Scolder, they're barking!" whispered Moldy.

"Not only that, they're very disobedient," said Scolder. "And their faces are so dirty! Speaking of dirt, did you notice how they were scratching—"

She realized her partner wasn't listening to her. He was staring, eyes wide, at something right outside the video arcade.

"What is it, Moldy?" Scolder asked. He didn't answer. Instead, he raced out of the arcade and into the mall as if he were trying to set a new world record for the one hundred-yard dash. Scolder ran after him, making her way through crowds of startled shoppers as quickly as she could. She could think of only one reason why Moldy had taken off at a run like that: He'd experienced another Sam sighting.

When she finally caught up with him at The Gap he was leaning against the front window, head pressed against the glass, eyes closed. Scolder's heart sank. He was crying.

"Moldy, here." She offered him a handkerchief. He blew his nose loudly.

"Scolder, I can't take much more of this," he said brokenly.

"I know it's hard on you." Scolder's voice was gentle, but there was a hint of surprise in it also. She'd never suspected just how tragic losing a pet could be. Poor Moldy.

"Just once," he moaned. "Just once I'd like to get here in time."

Now she was confused. Was he talking about his dog? "In time for what, Moldy?" she asked.

"In time for the sale!" he wailed. "I miss it EVERY SINGLE TIME! Do you know how disappointing that is?"

Scolder didn't respond. Was she thinking that her partner was a complete buffoon? Or teetering on the brink of insanity? Nobody would ever know from her expression.

"Moldy," she said at last, "there are lots of kids inside the store. Let's ask them some questions. Maybe they'll be more helpful than the first group." As she said this, a thought flickered at the edge of Scolder's mind, something about those kids in the arcade . . . the way they had looked . . . the way they'd behaved. . . . Before she could grasp it, the thought was gone.

So she followed Moldy into the store. He walked up to a group of kids who were trying on denim jackets, and said he'd like to ask them a few questions.

"What about?" sneered a girl who looked about fourteen years old. She cracked her gum so loudly that Scolder almost took cover. It sounded just like a pistol shot.

"Are you in the ninth grade?"

"Uh, yeah," said the girl. "So?"

"Did you do your homework last night?"

"Huh? No!" she answered. Two friends, a boy and a girl, sauntered over.

"Are you going to do it tonight?" asked Moldy.

"Not a chance," she said, blowing a huge bubble in his face. Her friends snickered.

"Me neither," agreed the boy, who wore a Beavis and Butt-Head T-shirt. "Homework sucks. Big time."

Moldy shot Scolder a meaningful look.

Their answers were just like the ones they'd gotten in the arcade! "What if," he said to the girl, "what if your parents said you had to do it?"

"Huh. Wouldn't." The girl scratched her arm.

The gesture caught Scolder's eye. Suddenly the thought that had been eluding her became clear. She stepped up to the girl, flashed her badge, and snapped, "FBI. Lose the gum! And let me see your arm."

"WOOF! Don't let her boss you around, Harmony Gail," said the other girl.

"WOOF! WOOF!" said the boy. "That badge is, like, probably a fake."

"YIP! YIP! It's cool, guys," said Harmony Gail, examining Scolder's badge. "Bad photo," she commented. "I like it." She pulled the gum out of her mouth until it was a thin pink string as long as her arm, which she extended right in front of Scolder.

The agent examined the girl's forearm

and saw that it was dotted with tiny little bumps.

Doona Scolder was a podiatrist, not a dermatologist. But she knew what those bumps were. "Flea bites!" she announced. "Look, Moldy." As he peered at them she said, "Those kids in the arcade were scratching, too. I'm sure of it."

"Are you saying they have flea bites also?" asked Moldy. "What if they're mosquito bites? Or the bites of some unknown alien creature so tiny, it can travel all over Cleveland completely undetected?"

"Mosquito season is over, Moldy," Scolder said patiently. "As for the bites coming from an alien creature, what evidence is there to support that theory?"

"Take another look at them, Scolder," said Moldy. "The bites are green, not pink. They're grouped in neat little circles, not random clusters, as if the creatures who made them were . . . were sending a highly encoded message in a transgalactic language! In short, Scolder," he said, "these are like no flea bites I've ever seen. And I've seen many," he added with a catch in his voice. "Sam had them before he . . . before he . . ." Tears welled up in Moldy's eyes.

"Who's Sam?" asked Harmony Gail, making a cat's cradle out of her gum.

"He was my dog," said Moldy, with an effort. "He's . . . lost."

"Oh, yeah?" said the boy, scratching an armpit. "Is he, like, a little gray dog that likes to hang around kids?"

Moldy's sad, tearful eyes lit up with interest. "Yes!" he cried. "I thought I saw him today— here, at the mall! Have you seen him, too?"

"Sure," said Harmony Gail. She paused just long enough to stick the stringy pink gum back into her mouth. "We call him Mall Mutt. He's kinda cute."

"Kinda weird, too," said the other girl, who had blue streaks in her hair.

"Weird?" asked Scolder. "What do you mean?"

"He's, you know, like a zombie," said the blue-haired girl.

"Totally," agreed Harmony Gail. She cracked her gum loudly and then blew a bubble as big as her face.

"Right," said the boy. "Big spooky eyes. Stiff little walk. Like he's hypnotized or something." Eyes wide and staring, the boy took a few stiff, mincing steps toward the agents. "Like that," he said.

"YIP! YIP!" barked Harmony Gail. "That's him exactly, Damion!"

"When was the last time you saw him?" asked Scolder.

"Two or three days ago," said Damion, scratching his armpit again.

"And how long have you had those bites?" she asked.

"Two or three days," he answered.

"Me, too," said Harmony Gail.

"WOOF!" barked her friend. "Me, too!"

The agents looked at each other. Then they stepped away from the ninth graders. "Scolder," said Moldy, "I know this sounds crazy, but bear with me." He took a deep breath. "I think there's a link between Sam and these kids. And I think their bites have something to do with it, too. Not only that, I think all of this is connected to the information Skunker gave us. Scolder," he went on, his eyes bright with excitement, "I think we're on the verge of cracking this case!"

Scolder shook her head. "That's impossible, Moldy."

"Why?" He was bewildered.

"No oozing," she said.

"Oozing?" he echoed.

"Nothing's oozed any gross disgusting smelly slime yet," she said patiently. "Or popped a giant mutant worm. Or exploded into lifelike blobs of squirming fleshy material. How can our case be solved?"

"Hmmm. I hate to admit it, but you're right, Scolder," said Moldy. Then he brightened. "Maybe we'll find something gross, disgusting, and smelly on Sam."

It was a thought he would soon regret.

The little dog could not ignore the alien voices coming from deep within his bristly gray coat. No. They commanded shrilly. And he had to obey. So he trotted past the video arcade, rode up the escalator, and passed The Gap. Seconds later he reached his destination: a crowded, noisy place that smelled of cheese, tomatoes, and unwashed teenagers—dozens of them.

The little dog slipped inside.

"Speaking of smelly," said Scolder as she and Moldy walked out of the store, "my nose tells me we're near a pizza parlor."

Moldy sniffed the air. "I hate to admit it,

but you're right, Scolder. Look!" He pointed. "There it is—Spooky's Pizza." They walked a little closer. "Funny name for a pizza place, but it smells good," said Moldy. "Hungry?" he asked his partner.

Her stomach growled. "Starved," she said. Dedicated as she was to the pursuit of truth, justice, and a rational explanation for every mystery, there was only one thing Doona Scolder wanted at that moment: a great big slice dripping with extra cheese.

They headed in.

Scolder never got her slice. Instead, she got something very unexpected: a small, gray, vacant-eyed schnauzer who just happened to be standing in her way as she rushed to the counter.

She got him because she tripped over him. And though a chorus of tiny alien fleas screamed at him to get away immediately, the little dog could not obey. How could he? Scolder was a hefty woman, and she was lying on top of him. The little dog could hardly breathe, much less move.

Scolder finally hoisted herself up, and the little dog took a deep breath. Then a man who looked strangely familiar lifted him up and hugged him so hard that once again the dog could hardly breathe.

Alien voices shrieked in alarm and commanded the dog to do their bidding. But it was hopeless.

Moldy had him now.

From the case notes of Doona Scolder:

Just three short days after the apprehension of Sam, Agent Molder's dog, ninth graders in Cleveland have exhibited a marked change in behavior. Once again they are polite, obedient, and

studious, doing their homework
and bathing daily. Their barking
has stopped as suddenly as it
began.

Assistant Director Skunker
seems pleased with the quick
resolution of this case; at
least he has stopped criticizing
the way I dress.

But there are questions about
Cleveland that linger. In my
opinion, there has been no
satisfactory explanation for the
dramatic change in its ninth
graders. Agent Moldy maintains
that it is the result of ridding
Sam of his many fleas. He is
convinced that the fleas were not
earthly creatures, but alien
beings, sent here to ruin our
young people by infecting them with
an obscure but virulent disorder,

Alienitis Disobedientitis.

Can this be proven? No. The dog, now clean, has regained his former lively manner, but a laboratory analysis of the fleas infesting him will never be done. Strangely, every single one of them disappeared during Sam's bath.

As a result, no evidence remains.

Were they truly alien fleas from another galaxy, as Moldy insists?

Or were they simply nasty little insects making a good dog miserable?

We will never know.

Meanwhile, this Hoax File is closed.

THE oaX FILES

#2: Ixnay on the Eezechay

"He's fine, Mom. Yes, much happier now that he's got his dog back. No, no. He's not married yet. Dating anybody? I don't think so." Holding the cordless phone to her ear, Doona Scolder opened her closet door while her mother kept talking. She looked inside the closet. There they were—her trusty bow and arrows. She was itching to pick them up. Sunday morning conversations with her mother, especially when they were full of hints about her unmarried partner, Wolf Moldy, always made Scolder want to shoot something.

"Sure, I will. Of course. Yes, I'll take care of myself. You, too, Mom. Love you. Bye."

Scolder hung up, frowning. She was a world-renowned podiatrist and a special agent for the FBI, but her mother still worried about her because she was single. It was hard to believe.

Scolder went back to her closet, picked up her bow, and looked at it thoughtfully. It felt good in her hands. Hefty. Solid. Capable of inflicting serious bodily harm. Target practice, she realized, would probably lift her spirits. There was nothing like hitting a bull's-eye to improve her mood—unless it was doing laser surgery on bunion clusters. The agent sighed. The good old days—the days of emergency bunion surgery—were over. Her work for the Bureau kept her far too busy for that.

"But I'll never be too busy to practice archery," she vowed. Within five minutes she was dressed and on her way to the woods.

At just about the same time, her partner, Special Agent Wolf Moldy, was driving full speed into the heart of the city. He was on his way to meet the man known as Sore Throat—or, as some called him, "Strep." Strep was the most mysterious person Moldy had ever met. He appeared out of the shadows at odd hours of the day and night. He said very little. And what he did say was so cryptic—and uttered in such a hoarse whisper—that it sometimes took Moldy months to figure out what he meant. At their last rendezvous he'd been almost completely silent, except for the moment he'd turned to Moldy and rasped, "Money is the eat of all roovil."

Moldy was still working on that one.

Not only were their encounters mysterious, there was always an element of danger involved in them, too. Strep was connected to the FBI somehow, and he'd warned Moldy that his information about the inner workings of the Bureau was so explosive that disclosure would result in World War III, the Apocalypse, and perhaps even the end of the Dewey Decimal System. He insisted on elaborate precautions for their meetings, which were always called at the last minute using a carrier pigeon and a car horn that played "Stairway to Heaven" outside Moldy's window.

But Moldy always agreed to meet Strep when he made contact, even if it was at some strange hour, in some hard-to-find, out-of-the-way place. It wasn't only that so much was at stake, though forestalling a global disaster was definitely a strong incentive. No. In addition to the highly classified information he passed on to Moldy, Strep always had some really good gossip.

What would it be today? Moldy was hoping that when they met, Strep would tell him what really happened when The Beatles split up.

Or something even more fascinating.

When Moldy reached the appointed meeting place—the Nutty Candy Mart, in Union Station—Strep was nowhere in sight. He was often late, so Moldy didn't worry. As a matter of fact, the agent was pleased—he'd never been to the Nutty Candy Mart before, and Strep's lateness would give him time to examine every single kind of gummi candy in the store.

Special Agent Wolf Moldy had a special fondness for gummi candies. Scolder liked to tease him about it. "You'll lose all your teeth if you keep eating them," she'd say. "And then YOU'LL be gummy."

Moldy's response was always the same: "Have one, Scolder, they're good for you."

Now he inspected the Nutty's display jars happily, marveling at the sheer number of gummi candies in the place. Staggering!

There were thirty-six by his count, everything from gummi worms to gummi bears to gummi nose dribbles in a brilliant shade of green. There were even some that were completely new to him, like pink gummi erasers and chocolate-covered gummi bears. Making a choice was going to be hard.

Should he stock up on his old favorite, rainbow gummi worms? Or try something new and different, like clear gummi mints? Just as Moldy was about to decide, he smelled something very pungent—ammonia?—and felt a tap on his shoulder.

It was Strep, wearing a long dark overcoat and a fuzzy plaid scarf. He'd wrapped the scarf around his neck so many times that it reached all the way to his mouth, partially covering it. As a result, Moldy had trouble hearing his greeting, which was uttered in a hoarse, gloomy whisper.

"Excuse me?" he asked.

"I said, 'Hello, Moldy,'" Strep rasped,

sidling over to him. As he did, the sharp scent Moldy had noticed earlier grew stronger, and his nose wrinkled. Before he could say a word, Strep thrust a small package wrapped in waxed paper at him.

"Ollofay the eezechay," he whispered solemnly, his red-rimmed eyes holding Moldy's in a stare heavy with meaning.

"Ollofay? What?" Moldy asked in confusion. The pungency of the smell made his nose run and his eyes water, and he was overwhelmed by a terrible fear. Had Strep for some reason handed him the scent glands of a skunk? Blinking uncontrollably, Moldy fished around in his pocket for a handkerchief and finally managed to blow his nose.

When he looked up, Strep was gone.

And he'd been left holding a piece of very smelly cheese.

Far from the Nutty Candy Mart, deep in a pine forest miles outside the city, Doona Scolder held up her bow. Breathing deeply, she tried to empty her mind of everything but the target thirty feet away, but nagging voices—her mother's, her boss Wally Skunker's—sounded in her head just loudly enough to be distracting. Trying to ignore them, she softened the focus of her eyes and took aim.

Then, drawing back her bowstring in a rapid, fluid gesture, she released her arrow. It flew straight and true, its bright red tail-feathers fiery against the blue sky. Scolder was pleased with the shot. *Bull's-eye!* she thought.

Then something happened that made Doona Scolder's strong yet graceful jaw drop in amazement. An arrow hit the bull's-eye. But it was not her arrow.

Her arrow was tipped with red feathers, and it had hit the target just slightly to the left of center. The arrow at the bullseye was tipped with purple feathers.

Scolder whirled around. A man—a tall man with long dark hair and intensely blue eyes—was standing quietly a few yards behind her. Where had he come from? It was as if he'd emerged from the woods like a tree spirit, thought Scolder. A very handsome tree spirit.

The man held a bow, and a quiver of purple-tipped arrows lay at his feet. They were beautiful feet, she noticed: long and slender, with well-articulated arches. Scolder blushed. She found certain kinds of feet very attractive, which was one reason why she sometimes missed podiatry.

There was a glint of amusement in the man's eyes as he nodded hello. Scolder's blush deepened. He wasn't handsome. He was devastating.

"Good shot," he said.

"Thanks," she replied. "Yours was, too."

"Years of practice." He stepped closer. A powerful, heady scent, like a hamster cage, only nicer, wafted Scolder's way. Her heart started beating much too loudly.

"Shoot here often?" he asked.

"I . . . I try to," she stammered. "I don't always have time, though."

"If you don't mind a word of advice...," he began, looking deep into her eyes.

"No! No, of course not," she said, transfixed.

"Your form is excellent. However, I sense a wavering in your concentration. As if you are distracted by internal chatter."

Scolder was dumbfounded. How did he know that?

"Concentration is important in many things. In archery it is essential," the man went on. He picked up his quiver. "Improving your concentration would make all the difference." As he said this, he fixed her with a look so intense that her body temperature jumped by several degrees. "You could compete," he added, handing her a card. It read:

WILLIAM DEMIGOD, I.A.

(607) 555-2708

ARCHER, SHAMAN,

CERTIFIED PUBLIC ACCOUNTANT

"MY AIM IS TRUE"

Scolder didn't recognize the area code. And the little cactuses on the card made her willing to bet that William Demigod was not a local resident.

"You're visiting from . . . ?" she asked.

"New Mexico," he replied. "Give me a call if you come out that way." With just the hint of a smile he added, "We can work on your concentration."

Before she could reply, he'd turned and melted into the woods. Scolder watched him go, her bow and arrows forgotten.

William Demigod was in for a surprise, she thought. In less than a week she'd be attending her cousin Harriet's wedding in New Mexico. Until today, Scolder hadn't been looking forward to the event. In fact, she'd only agreed to go as a favor to Harriet.

Now wild horses couldn't keep her away.

"You know I hate to leave you, Sammy," Wolf Moldy said to his little gray schnauzer. "But it's only for a few days. And you'll be at the FBI kennel. Only very special dogs get to stay there."

Sam looked up at him from under his bushy eyebrows, his dark eyes bright with curiosity, and wagged his stubby little tail. Moldy felt a pang of guilt. True, the Bureau kennel was state of the art. Its sleek, carefully monitored dog dorms offered everything from holographic fire hydrants to *Free Willy* videos. And its staff was extraordinarily well qualified; many were doctoral candidates in animal pharmaceuticals or canine grooming. Yet it was a struggle for Moldy to give Sam over to their care. He and his dog had been apart for so long. It didn't seem right for them to separate yet again.

On the other hand, he just couldn't ignore the calls he'd gotten that morning. The first was from Wally Skunker, ordering him to fly out to New Mexico right away to join Scolder. "I'll give it to you straight," he'd told Moldy. "If this isn't a Hoax File, I'm buying myself a ponytail hat."

The second was from Scolder herself. What she'd reported to Moldy—about the arrow in the desert, the hidden chamber in the canyon, and her discovery of a mysterious cheeselike substance there—sounded like a case that only the two of them could solve.

Moldy patted Sam's head. "I'll send you a postcard," he promised.

The wedding was fun, Scolder wrote on a postcard to her mother, *and Harriet's husband seems very nice. When she told him I was a podiatrist he asked me dozens of questions about foot health. Turns out he sells shoes for a living! I'm enjoying New Mexico, especially the desert. Went hiking yesterday and found some really interesting animal remains—a prairie dog, a rattlesnake, and an iguana (I think). Call you when I'm back. XOXO Doona.*

Scolder addressed the card and sighed. Her mother would be pleased with what she'd written, though it was far from the truth. Not that Scolder had really lied in the postcard. She had enjoyed Harriet's wedding, and finding those animal skeletons really had been a thrill. But other aspects of her trip had been disappointing—if not downright bizarre—and she had no intention of sharing them with her mother.

William Demigod, for example. Scolder had called the mysterious archer as soon as she'd arrived, and he'd sounded genuinely pleased to hear from her, quickly suggesting that they meet up on Sunday, the day after the wedding. Scolder had just as quickly agreed. He was going to pick her up at five so they could drive into the desert for the sunset. It had sounded very romantic. Scolder had been looking forward to it.

And then he hadn't shown up. Scolder had waited for half an hour, then an hour. Finally she'd called his number, only to get a recording saying that it was no longer in service.

Strange. And disappointing. But what followed was stranger still.

She'd decided to visit the desert on her own. Why not drive out there in her rental car with her trusty bow and arrows? Shooting at a few cactuses might cheer her up.

Or so she'd thought.

Instead, one of her arrows had gone astray. It had led her into a canyon, and from there. . . .

Scolder's nose wrinkled as she glanced over at the motel minibar. Inside the tiny refrigerator was a package—one she'd wrapped carefully, and then surrounded with ice cubes. She'd done everything she could to mask its smell.

But she hadn't been entirely successful.

Because the thing *reeked*. Its odor was so strong that she'd kept the car windows wide open on the drive back from the desert. And even on ice, stashed in the minibar, its smell had crept into the room. Pungent. Biting. Powerful. *Like the smelliest foot in the universe,* thought Scolder, *or the worst fungus ever to afflict humankind—E. Toenailitis Putriditis.* She stuffed a pair of cotton balls into her nostrils.

Then she checked her watch anxiously:

11 A.M. Moldy was flying in today from Washington. He was due in an hour.

It would be a relief to see him, she thought, a relief to compare . . . specimens and try to figure what they were, and if they were related.

Meanwhile, she stuffed some more cotton into her nose.

And prayed there wouldn't be a power failure.

Thousands of miles away, the man called Sore Throat sat alone in his apartment, drinking cough medicine out of the bottle and staring at a photograph. It was a picture of a blond, teenage, shirtless boy who wore a feather in his long matted hair, several strands of beads, and moccasins. He was making a peace sign at the camera and laughing uproariously, as if he'd just heard a particularly hilarious joke.

Or ingested some illegal substance.

Sore Throat, on the other hand, was not laughing. He was not even smiling. All the cough medicine in the world couldn't ease his pain.

"Cloud," he whispered, his face twisted with anguish, "forgive me. I had to do it. I had no choice."

"Ollofay the WHAT?" Scolder exclaimed. "You mean he talked to you in pig latin? That's insane!" She and her partner were sitting in the motel coffee shop, and Moldy was filling her in on his meeting with Sore Throat.

"Superficially, perhaps, Scolder," Moldy replied calmly, popping a gummi nose dribble into his mouth. He washed it down with some herbal tea and made a discreet sound of enjoyment. "But a brilliant mind like mine, which is more than capable of sorting out the wheat of meaning from the chaff of nonsense—if you'll allow me to speak metaphorically, and, after all, what choice do you have?—has already detected the method to Sore Throat's madness."

He popped another nose dribble and paused dramatically. Scolder waited for him to go on. Did she think her partner sounded like a jerk? Did she want to scream, "Get to the point, already!"? If so, her expression did not betray it.

"I believe that Sore Throat's use of pig latin was involuntary," said Moldy. "That means he didn't want to use it, Scolder. But he had to. Because there's a connection—an important connection—between the reeking, stinking, grossly smelly piece of cheese he gave me and that obscure language. And that connection was very much on his mind when we met."

"But—" Scolder began, every molecule of her rational being recoiling from this off-the-wall theory.

"Don't interrupt, Scolder. You know I'm right," said Moldy. "I always am."

The truth was, thought Scolder, that Moldy was always *partially* right, but sometimes the ratio of his rightness to his wrongness was very small. Like 1 to 100. Besides, she was in no mood to argue. They still had to compare specimens. And that was going to be an ordeal. So she said nothing.

"Anyway," continued Moldy, "why don't we compare specimens? Maybe run some tests on them? The results may lead us to a place where pig latin is spoken. Or otnay," he added with a grin.

Scolder got up from the table. "Soundsay oodgay," she replied with just the hint of a smile.

Five minutes later, though, neither she nor Moldy was smiling. Now their faces were dead serious, even grim. For the smell that assailed their nostrils in Room 552 of the Big Butte Motor Inn was enough to make strong agents weep.

Which they were.

"AAGH!" exclaimed Moldy, choking and wiping tears from his eyes. "I thought *my* cheese was stinky. Yours is nerve gas, Scolder!"

"I know," she replied, blowing her nose. "Mine must be a purer form. Or more concentrated."

The agents compared the two pieces of cheese, which were sitting side by side on the bureau. They were both crumbly, greenish, and shot with streaks of a pale silvery color. And they both stank.

"This is like no cheese on earth," muttered Moldy. "I wonder... where did you say you found it?" he asked Scolder.

"In the desert," she said, "when I was shooting. My arrow flew into a canyon, and when I chased it down, I found a passageway hidden in the rocks. Naturally I had to investigate. The smell put me off at first, but my curiosity won out." She pointed at her piece of cheese. "This came from a huge mound of the stuff," she said. "Sitting in a kind of rock chamber at the end of the passageway. I couldn't tell if there was anything else in there—it was too dark."

"You didn't have your flashlight with you?" Moldy sounded shocked.

"I was practicing archery, Moldy," Scolder said as patiently as she knew how. "Normally that requires a bow and some arrows—not a flashlight."

"Hmm. Right. Well, we've got to go back there," said her partner. "With a flashlight. Which I just happen to have," he added smugly.

Scolder waited. She knew there was more.

She was right.

"I have a feeling this cheese is highly unusual," Moldy went on. "Perhaps even the key to a major discovery of potentially earth-shaking importance. By the way, you don't happen to have a gas mask, do you? Or some clothespins?"

Scolder shook her head. "I came here for a wedding, Moldy," she reminded him. "I packed a dress and heels. Call me crazy, but the occasion didn't seem to call for a gas mask."

"We're going to need something to protect us against that smell," he said.

"You're right," Scolder agreed. "But all I have is these." She showed him the cotton balls.

"I guess they'll have to do." Moldy took a handful as Scolder put the two pieces of cheese back into the minibar.

"Eddyray?" he asked her.

"Eddyray," she replied.

And then the phone rang. Scolder was surprised. Who could be calling her here at the motel? Harriet was in Bali on her honeymoon, Moldy was standing next to her. . . . She picked up and heard a deep male voice say, "Doona Scolder?"

"Who's calling, please?" she asked.

"It's William Demigod. I'm very sorry I missed our meeting yesterday," he added quickly. "There was some urgent tribal business, and I just couldn't get away."

"It must have been very urgent," said Scolder. "Your phone's been disconnected."

"Yes, I know," he said, sounding both troubled and reluctant to say more. In the brief silence that followed Scolder wondered what tribe he belonged to. He certainly didn't look Native American.

She glanced over at Moldy. He was standing at the door watching her, waiting. Suddenly their mission to investigate the mysterious cheese in the desert seemed a lot more compelling than talking to a guy who'd just stood her up. No matter how pretty his feet were.

"Look," she said into the receiver, "I was just going out. Is there a number where I can reach you?"

"Of course," he said, giving her the number. "Promise you'll call."

"I promise," said Scolder, hanging up.

"Do you always cross your fingers when you say that?" teased Moldy.

"I say eway etlay emthay ogay."

"I say eway eepkay emthay! At least until the Eefchay etsgay erehay."

"Ohnay away!"

"Esyay!"

"Ohnay!"

Moldy and Scolder listened to this exchange in silence. They had no choice but to listen in silence, because one short hour after leaving the motel they were bound and gagged. And their captors—two teenage boys wearing face paint, feathers, and beads—were arguing about what to do with them. In very high, squeaky voices. In pig latin.

They sounded like demented chipmunks and they looked like rejects from a Halloween parade, but the two young men had ambushed and captured them with embarrassing ease. Moldy and Scolder hadn't even had time to get a good look at the entry room—the room with the cheese in it—before they were overpowered.

And now they were prisoners in some kind of underground storehouse. Three candles cast just enough light so that they could see each other, their captors, and stacks of metal tanks lining the walls. Their noses told them they were far from the entry room.

Their instincts told them they could be in terrible danger.

Their stomachs told them they were hungry.

Moldy and Scolder looked at each other. Their gags might keep them from speaking, but their working relationship was so close that they could communicate without words.

Now a glance passed between them.

A glance full of meaning.

Scolder's look meant, *Did I really give an attractive man with beautiful feet the brush-off for this, after he called to apologize? My mother would never forgive me if she knew.*

Moldy's look meant, *Even though I'm bound and gagged, my brilliant mind is formulating an escape plan, devising a strategy to end world hunger, and trying very hard to remember if I paid my last phone bill.*

Scolder was wondering if Moldy's plan to end world hunger included gummi candy, when her attention was drawn to the far end of the room, where a tall, long-haired man appeared from the shadows. As he came closer she saw his feet. They were long and slender and unusually beautiful.

With a shock she recognized William Demigod.

"Eefchay!" squeaked one of the boys on seeing Demigod. "Eerhay they arehay!" He pointed to Moldy and Scolder.

Eefchay? thought Scolder. Of *utway?*

"Doona!" exclaimed Demigod. "What are *you* doing here?"

Scolder gave him a look that said, *I'd tell you, but there's a gag in my mouth.*

Fortunately he understood. "Untie her!" he snapped. "And get that gag out of her mouth—ownay!" As soon as his men obeyed, Demigod helped Scolder to her feet. "Now," he said, "what *are* you doing here?"

"I could ask you the same question," said Scolder, dusting herself off. "And lots of others, too. Who are you, anyway? Why are you and your friends dressed up like Indians? How come you're talking pig latin? Do you have any pretzels? And would you mind taking off your moccasins?"

Before Demigod could reply, a muffled sound of protest came from the ground. It was Moldy, who was still bound and gagged. Scolder had forgotten about him.

"Oh, uh, this is my partner, Wolf Moldy," she added. "Would you please untie him also?"

"Before I do, you must give me your solemn promise not to reveal what you learn here," said Demigod.

"Why should I do that?" asked Scolder.

"The fate of my tribe—the Igpay Atinlay—depends on it," said Demigod.

"Oh, okay," said Scolder. "I promise."

From his place on the floor, Moldy could see that Scolder was crossing her fingers behind her back. *She's a sly one!* he thought admiringly.

"And you? Do you promise?" Demigod asked Moldy. Moldy nodded, and was freed. As he stood, he and Scolder quickly made eye contact.

They telegraphed a message to each other: *Smelly cheese! Pig latin! Bogus tribe! Major revelation on the way!*

Demigod's men led the two agents into yet another room. This one, lit by kerosene lamps, was filled with rows of chairs lined up in front of a small platform that looked like a stage. *It's almost like a cabaret theater,* thought Moldy, feeling a thrill of foreboding. *Strange.*

"Itsay," squeaked the blond one, whose face suddenly looked oddly familiar to Moldy. He could swear he'd seen the boy before. But where?

They sat.

William Demigod climbed onto the platform and sat down cross-legged. The boys joined him. One carried a drum. The other—the blond—held a banjo.

Moldy paled. His instincts had been right. He was in danger.

Moldy had managed to hide his deep

aversion to banjo music for most of his professional life. The truth was that it made him ill and delirious. Only Scolder knew. She'd found out last year, during their work on the Mutant Hootenanny Hoax File, when Moldy had suffered a brief mental collapse during an intense round of dueling banjos.

Scolder looked over at him with pity in her eyes. This was going to be an ordeal for him. But there was nothing she could do.

William Demigod looked at the agents solemnly. He told them they were about to hear "The Song of the Green Cheese Moon," a sacred legend of his tribe. The banjo player strummed a chord. The drummer beat out a slow, steady rhythm on the conga. And Demigod sang:

"When the world was young
So very long ago
At the dawn of time
At the beginning of life

The heavens were in flux
The movies were in black and white
And Earth was lonely
Yes, she was very lonely
She was so very lonely.
For Earth had no friends
No neighbors, no kids
No pets or dependents
Not even a houseplant
She needed a moon.
She needed a moon.
Oh, yes, she needed a moon!
Oh, yes, she needed a moon!
Earth looked for a moon
She looked high and low
She asked the sun
She consulted the stars
She shopped for weeks
She advertised
She needed a moon!
Oh, yes, she needed a moon!
One day out of the blue

A moon appeared for Earth
A green moon for Earth
It was the color of grass
It was the color of peas
The color of money
The color of cheese
The color of mold
The color of moss
The color of unwaxed peppermint floss
It was a green cheese moon
It was a green cheese moon
Oh, yes, a green cheese moon."

Moldy twitched every time the banjo player strummed his instrument. Scolder knew he was in agony. She wasn't doing too well, either. The drummer was terrible. And William Demigod's voice was affecting her ears the way that cheese had affected her nose.

Please let him stop singing soon, she prayed. Every ounce of her enthusiasm about the case, her curiosity about the secrets of the canyon, even her admiration for William Demigod's handsome feet, was gone, replaced by an urgent need to get out of this place and hunker down with a burger and some fries.

Demigod stopped singing.

Scolder's heart leaped with joy—too soon. He was only pausing briefly to pick up a recorder. Closing his eyes, he raised it to his lips and blew three cruelly piercing notes. The drummer beat his drum as if he were trying to pound it into the center of the earth. And the banjo player struck a chord with such force that it bounced off the rock walls, made straight for Moldy and Scolder's quivering brains like a heat-seeking missile, and exploded there with excruciating loudness.

Demigod resumed his song:

> *"The earth was so happy*
> *She—"*

Moldy leaped to his feet with sweat pouring down his face. "Stop! Stop!" he screamed. "Please, no more! Let us out of here! We'll do anything! Anything you want!" He turned to Scolder. "We will, Doona," he cried, his voice cracking, "won't we?"

Scolder's self-control was the stuff of legends, described in hushed, reverential tones at the Bureau by even the most hard-bitten investigators. Supremely disciplined and self-possessed, she inspired admiration mixed with fear—for she had never cracked, never even come close to giving up on a case until it was solved. Some called it "tensile strength." Some called it "old-fashioned willpower." Some called it "disestablishmentarianism," but they were wrong.

Whatever it was, it had given her an enviable record, with a reputation to match.

Was the renowned podiatrist-turned-agent about to change all that just because of some really bad music? She looked at William Demigod, who raised his recorder to his mouth and puckered his lips.

That was all it took. "Yes," she said. "We'll do anything."

"Promise?" asked Demigod.

"Promise," she answered. And this time she didn't cross her fingers.

A change in Demigod's expression told the two boys to put down their instruments. Moldy whimpered with relief, and Scolder let out a sigh. Then they followed Demigod back to the room lined with metal tanks, where the boys retreated into a shadowy corner. Moldy heard a whooshing sound and then a squeak, but he couldn't make out what they were doing.

Especially when Demigod was so intent on telling them about his tribe. "The Igpays are a peace-loving people," he announced. "United by respect for nature, allegiance to the mother tongue, and a belief in the healing properties of the elements."

"The healing properties of the elements?" asked Scolder, her scientific curiosity aroused. "You mean the benefits of fresh air and saltwater?"

"Not exactly," said Demigod. "Just one element, a gaseous—"

He was interrupted by a high-pitched giggle from the corner, which was followed by a peal of squeaky laughter.

"Gaseous?" Hearing the laughter, Moldy's powers of analysis, deadened by banjo music, revived. "Helium!" he exclaimed. "The gaseous element he's talking about is helium, Scolder! They're inhaling it! That's why they sound so funny!"

Scolder realized that for once Moldy was absolutely right. The boys, crouched beside a metal tank, were taking deep breaths out of a couple of inflated balloons and giggling like tipsy squirrels.

Scolder looked inquiringly at Demigod.

"It is a tribal ritual," he told her. "The Igpays believe that Moon Gas—"

"MOON gas?" Moldy echoed.

"—was left here for a purpose. Our tribal elders found it long ago. They knew they must guard it. For the gas is holy," continued Demigod.

"Holy? Why?" asked Scolder.

"It allows us to communicate directly with the cosmos."

"By squeaking? Now I've heard everything," said Moldy. He turned to Scolder. "And you call *my* ideas far-fetched?"

The blond boy walked over and offered a balloon to Moldy. "Eacepay, udeday," he squeaked with a grin.

"Cloud—" said Demigod, as if warning the boy away.

Moldy peered into the boy's face. Those

eyes...that nose.... He'd seen them before, he was certain. But where? When? And then Moldy knew. Take away the boy's braids and his face paint, add thirty years, a shapeless gray overcoat, and a muffler and he would be—Strep!

Was Cloud Strep's son? If so, he could be the reason for Strep's bizarre utterance— "ollofay the eezechay"—and the hunk of smelly cheese he'd passed to Moldy at the Nutty Candy Mart last week! Strep wanted Moldy to find his son!

Like iron filings clamping onto a magnet, all the tiny, seemingly disparate bits of this maddeningly difficult case came together for Moldy. A million-watt flash of insight made clear the connections between Cloud, Strep, William Demigod, Scolder, the canyon, gummi candies, green cheese, the moon, helium, and every other part of the universe, whether large, small, or economy-sized.

"Incredible!" he shouted.

Startled, Scolder jumped. "What's incredible?" she asked. Few things had ever frightened her as much as the possibility of hearing Demigod sing again, and she'd been eyeing him warily, terrified that he'd decide it was time for another verse of "The Song of the Green Cheese Moon."

But Moldy's cry of amazement distracted her, and her concentration broke for an instant.

That was all it took.

When they regained consciousness the agents were in their rental car, parked beside a silent desert road. It was night. "Moldy, where are we?" asked Scolder, shaking her head to clear it. "What happened?"

He peered outside. "Looks like the desert," he said. "As for what happened, all I remember is looking at that blond kid's face and thinking he reminded me of somebody. . . ."

"You shouted," said Scolder. "You shouted, 'Incredible!'"

"Did I?" Moldy scratched his head. "It's all so hazy. I think they drugged us, Scolder."

"I think so, too," she agreed. "With something a lot stronger than helium."

They climbed out of the car. A billion stars twinkled. The moon beamed down at them from the vast Western sky, looking for all the world like a hunk of green cheese. The wind, cool now that it was night, whispered brokenly of secrets and promises.

A low rumble, like the voice of some mysterious desert god, broke the silence. It was Scolder's stomach. "God, I'm starving!" she cried. "Let's get out of here and eat something!"

Moldy smiled. "As long as it isn't cheese," he said.

From the case notes of Doona Scolder:

Moldy's many attempts to
contact Strep have so far been
unsuccessful. Until Strep once
again makes himself available
to us, we will not know just
why he gave Moldy that cheese.
We may never know.

Consequently, the results
of our investigation have been
poor. We have wasted time,
money, and energy on a wild-
goose chase in the desert. I
have lost an excellent bow and
several very expensive arrows.
Moldy is now allergic to cheese.
Skunker laughed at our account

of the trip and has been making
crude jokes in pig latin ever
since.

And my mother keeps asking
if I met any single men at the
wedding.

There is only one positive
thing that can be said about
this case. For now, this Hoax
File is closed.

THE hoaX FILES

#3: Epidermis Enigmata

"Are you sure, Dr. Blotchmore?" Nick Jackson was a big, muscular sixteen-year-old, but he sounded small and uncertain as he got up from the doctor's examination bench. This pleased Rufus Blotchmore: He liked his teenage patients insecure. They were more profitable that way.

"Of course, I'm sure," the doctor replied with calculated heartiness, clapping Nick's broad shoulder. "Just go easy on the fried foods and chocolate, wash your face twice a day, and use the cream religiously. Every night! No cheating, understand?"

Nick nodded.

Poor desperate pimply fool, thought the

doctor. "Good! I'll check on you in a month," he said, ushering Nick out. *And the month after that, and the month after that,* he thought, strolling into his own office and picking up the telephone. *Because—fortunately for me—there's no quick cure for acne. Especially with my special slow-acting, secret formula ointment.*

He dialed. "Hello, Eloise," he said, when his travel agent picked up. "Dr. Blotchmore here. Fine, fine. Listen, would you book me onto that golf cruise to the Islands? I've decided to go after all. Um-hmm, first class." He chuckled. "Yes, business is good. No complaints."

The doctor hung up. *God bless my teenage patients,* he thought, *and every zit and pustule on their sad, self-conscious faces.*

The intercom on his desk buzzed. "Yes?"

"Your three-fifteen is here, doctor."

"Be right out," he called, swinging an imaginary golf club.

It would be nice to get away.

Chris Flartenberg looked at his reflection in the bathroom mirror and winced. His skin, covered with bright pink blemishes, made him so self-conscious that he could barely stand to look at it.

But I have to, he thought. *At least tonight.* It was February thirteenth, Jennifer Jackson's birthday, and tonight was her combination birthday–Valentine's Day party. She'd invited everyone in their class.

Even me, thought Chris. He had a furious crush on Jennifer, though they'd barely spoken. He'd wanted to, of course, but since he'd broken out he'd been too self-conscious to talk to her, even when she smiled at him. The thought of seeing her tonight made his head buzz.

Facing his reflection with a mixture of disgust and self-pity, Chris wondered for the thousandth time why this had happened to him. He didn't deserve all these big red pimples, especially when everyone else in his family had normal skin. His know-it-all sister, Fifi, had never had a single pimple in her life, which was grossly unfair.

"Life isn't fair, Chris." That's what his mother always said when he complained about his skin. The last time she'd uttered the words, he'd flushed angrily, wishing that a big red pimple would appear on her face—just so she'd know how it felt. Now all he wished was that a miracle would happen and his skin would clear up, so he'd have the courage to talk to Jennifer.

Sighing, he picked up a well-squeezed tube of Oxy 10.

It was time to get ready for the party.

Special FBI Agent Doona Scolder glanced at her reflection in the mirror casually and then did a double take. She leaned forward to examine her face more closely. There, just next to her left nostril, was a small red blemish.

Scolder frowned. *A pimple? I haven't had a pimple since I was thirteen!* But there it was, staring back at her. *Must have been the fried calamari I ate last night,* she thought, *and all that chocolate mousse. Bad combination. Delicious, though.*

Scolder loved food almost as much as she loved her work for the Bureau. She kept trim, despite a healthy appetite, because her job as a special agent was so physically strenuous. She and Wolf Moldy worked twelve- and fourteen-hour shifts. They often ran miles at a stretch in pursuit of suspects. Sometimes they had to climb fences or wade through large bodies of water or run up the "down" escalators, shouting, "Stop! FBI!" The pace was fast—much faster than when Scolder had spent all her time examining problem feet. Though she sometimes missed the measured calm of podiatry, Scolder would never ever miss being twenty pounds heavier.

Now she found some concealer in her makeup drawer and dabbed at the blemish. The act brought back a flood of memories from her teenage years, when she'd worried constantly that her skin would never clear up.

Torment cake with agony icing, she thought with a shudder. *Thank God those days are over*.

Doona Scolder was in for a surprise.

Chris Flartenberg checked to make sure that the bathroom door was locked, and then opened the medicine cabinet. He could hear loud music and the roar of forty-odd classmates talking, drinking, dancing, flirting, and trying to look cool. From the sound of it, they were having a good time.

He wasn't.

The trouble had started even before he'd arrived. A violent thunderstorm had caught him on his walk over, and he'd shown up soaking wet, his hair plastered down, and his clothes clinging to his body. When he'd walked into the Jacksons' house, Annie Tworkov had stared at him and whispered something to Celia Barton, who'd promptly started giggling. From the way they were act-ing he'd figured he looked ridiculous, which had made him blush furiously. Then the birthday girl, Jennifer, appeared, greeting him with a big smile, but she'd gotten dragged away by a bunch of kids before he could even mumble a response. *So much for talking to her*, he'd thought bitterly.

He'd stood near the kitchen unnoticed as his classmates jostled past him to get at the food. Soon he'd started wondering which was worse: too much attention, or too little. When Hannah Butler, official class geek, planted herself next to him and started babbling about the knitting symbolism in *A Tale of Two Cities*, he'd decided that too much attention was definitely worse.

That was when he'd retreated to the upstairs bathroom.

Now here he was, looking through the medicine cabinet. He wasn't sure why. He certainly wasn't interested in taking any drugs, though there was quite a selection in the cabinet—everything from Prozac to Zoloft to Zyban.

Is that why she's always so cheerful? thought Chris, seeing Jennifer's name on many of the vials. Judging from the electric razor and the Black & Decker aftershave, her brother Nick shared the bathroom with her, though Jennifer's makeup and perfume took up most of the shelf space.

An array of skin-care products on the bottom shelf caught Chris's eye. Clearasil,

Oxy 10, Differin, and a silver tube with DR. RUFUS BLOTCHMORE, DERMATOLOGY on the label. He picked up the tube. The prescription, a benzoyl peroxide ointment, was for Nicholas Jackson. *Of course*, thought Chris. *Nick has acne, too. Not as bad as I do, though*.

Chris wondered if the prescription ointment was better than the over-the-counter ones. *Duh*, he thought, *it has to be. I bet it's a million times stronger*. He opened the tube, and a squiggle of clear ointment hurried onto his finger, as if asking to be used.

Chris wasn't about to say no. He rubbed the ointment all over his face and neck, liking the way it tingled on his skin. It felt surprisingly good—much better than anything he'd ever tried. He closed his eyes. *If only it worked. Right away, so his skin was completely clear when he opened his eyes—*

There was a knock on the door, and a girl's voice called, "What are you doing in there?" Chris's eyes flew open. There was another knock, louder this time. "Hey, man! Did you fall in?"

Chris closed the tube hastily and stuck it in his pocket. "Be right out," he called, running the water in the sink for a moment. When he opened the door, Annie Tworkov and Celia Barton were leaning against the wall.

"Sorry to disturb you," said Annie, sounding far from sorry. Celia snickered, following Annie into the bathroom and slamming the door. Chris stood there for a moment feeling agitated. He'd never stolen anything before, and he still wasn't sure why he'd taken that tube of ointment. One thing he did know: It was time to leave the party. Running into Nick Jackson now would be just too weird.

A sweet, pungent smell drifted out of the bathroom, followed by the sound of giggling. Annie and Celia were smoking grass.

Is that why they're always acting so stupid? wondered Chris. The door opened, and they tumbled out.

"Whoops!" shrieked Annie, practically tripping over him. "Watch it!" She teetered on her platform soles and grabbed Celia's arm, throwing Celia off balance.

"Yeah, Zit Boy, look out," snapped Celia. She glared at him, her pupils wide, her mouth a disapproving purple squiggle.

Chris didn't say anything. *Zit Boy? Who was she to call him names?* A wave of anger, more intense than any he'd ever felt before, coursed through him, turning his face rose-red and his eyes into slits that flashed like warning lights. Mixed with his rage was an odd sense of detachment, as if he were high above the hallway, looking down at a scene staged especially for his benefit.

Despite the dim light he could see everything with absolute clarity: the wallpaper, the bird prints in their gilt frames, the banister, and the two glassy-eyed girls looking at him with annoyance.

And then, as he watched, their expressions changed—first to surprise, then to something more like fear. "Oh, my god," blurted Annie, "look at his face!"

Chris realized that his face was tingling again. The feeling was stronger now, but it didn't hurt—it actually felt better than when he'd first applied Dr. Blotchmore's ointment.

Celia's eyes widened. "I don't believe it!" She turned to her friend. "Are we, like, having hallucinations?" she asked, her voice shaking.

"I don't know," Annie said nervously. "It was just normal weed."

"I knew I shouldn't have smoked it!" moaned Celia, still staring at Chris. "Shut up, Cee!" hissed Annie. "Cool it!" She dug a pocket mirror out of her shoulder bag and offered it to Chris. "Here," she said. "Take a look at yourself."

Chris took the mirror. He looked at his reflection. And blinked.

His skin was perfectly clear.

He stood there, knowing that some kind of miracle had been performed, and the sheer wonder of it made him dizzy. Examining his perfect complexion with grateful tears welling up in his eyes, he suddenly experienced an emotion as powerful as it was new.

He felt the desire to help others.

Chris looked at Celia, who was still staring at him with her mouth hanging open. He noticed there was a large pimple on her chin. "Step closer," he said, his voice quiet but firm. She approached him unsteadily, clutching her velour-clad middle.

Chris's hand reached out to her face. Closing his eyes, he summoned up all the relief and gratitude he'd felt when he'd first seen his newly clear complexion. He let it wash over him in a great cleansing wave. As it did, he touched Celia's pimple.

He let his hand rest there for a moment and then drew it away. When he opened his eyes her expression was dazed—and her skin was perfectly clear. Chris smiled. Celia turned to Annie questioningly.

"Oh, my God," moaned her friend. "I can't believe it! Look in the mirror, Cee."

Chris gave Celia the mirror. He watched, smiling, as a look of pure joy spread over her face.

This party might turn out to be okay after all.

My skin was perfectly clear this morning, thought Wolf Moldy, staring into his bathroom mirror at the strange new spot on his face. *What happened?* He searched his mind for clues.

The day had been unremarkable: a ten-mile predawn run, followed by three hours of yoga, meditation, and astral projection. A meeting with Wally Skunker to discuss the annual J. Edgar Hoover Look-alike Contest. Lunch—the usual vegetables, brown rice, and gummi candy—followed by a walk with his beloved dog, Sam. An afternoon training session with rookies, viewing and comparing both versions of *Invasion of the Body Snatchers.* His usual dinner of tofu, brown rice, and gummi candy. A brief conversation with his partner, Doona Scolder. And a late-night phone session with his private psychic, Claire Voyance.

Where did this pimple come from? And why didn't Claire predict it? Could she be slipping up? thought Moldy. A thrill of fear coursed through his body like a gerbil on a fun run. He shuddered.

Many things puzzled Wolf Moldy. Many things fascinated him. Some things repulsed him, and a few made him sneeze uncontrollably. But few things frightened him like the appearance of an unsightly blemish on his face. He had seen enough unsightly blemishes in his career—blemishes caused by supernatural forces, blemishes that hid extraterrestrial beings, blemishes with the ability to think, speak, even read minds—to view this one with equanimity.

He shuddered again.

Extreme measures were required.

He'd have to call The Secretives.

The Secretives, three friends who knew more about accessing information—no matter how obscure—than any other people Moldy had ever met, worked out of a typewriter repair shop on the edge of the city. Like Moldy, they had an intense distrust of authority. Unlike him, they were virtually unemployable, thanks to their ignorance of normal personal hygiene and their lack of social skills. But it didn't matter to Moldy that they wore their pajamas to work, or smelled like a turkey farm, or held a daily belching contest—they were brilliant. And he trusted them. They'd supplied him with vital information many times.

He dialed their number and hung up on the first ring. He dialed again, let the phone ring twice, and hung up. He dialed a third time, let the phone ring three times, and waited.

Someone picked up. "Papa oo mao mao," pronounced a man's voice.

"Papa oo mao mao mao," replied Moldy. There was a brief silence.

"Moldy? What's up?"

"I need your help, Stan."

"You got it."

Moldy breathed a long sigh of relief. And then he told Secretive Stan why he was calling.

He looked in the mirror and breathed a long, ragged sigh of relief, then whispered a silent prayer of thanks to whatever mysterious god had performed the miracle. Two weeks after the party, his skin was still clear. More miraculous still, his power to heal had remained with him. Once word of it had spread—and it had spread fast, thanks to Celia and Annie—the complexion-impaired had begun to seek him out.

At first he saw them individually.

As their numbers grew, it became necessary to see them in groups.

At the latest meeting he'd cured Nick Jackson, Andrea Reed, and the McGee twins, Hamish and Hamilton. In the rejoicing that followed, Nick had offered Chris his services as a bodyguard, Andrea had told him she'd do his Latin homework for the rest of the year, and Jenny Jackson had agreed to go out with him.

For the first time in a very long time, life was good.

Dr. Rufus Blotchmore adjusted his new palm-tree bow tie, sat down at his desk, and buzzed his nurse. He was eager to get back to working—and making money—after his very nice but very expensive golf cruise. "Susan," he said, admiring his tan in the mirror behind his chair, "when's my first appointment?"

"You don't have anything until two," she replied.

"Two?" He checked his watch. "It's only ten o'clock! I thought I was booked through the morning."

Though his nurse disliked him intensely, even she couldn't help feeling sorry for him at this moment. "They've all canceled, Doctor," she said.

"Canceled? What? Are you sure? There must be some mistake!" He stood up. "Who canceled?" he demanded.

"Nick Jackson, the McGee boys—" At that moment the phone rang. "Excuse me,

Doctor, " she said. "I should get this."

"Leave it on speaker," he barked. "I want to listen."

"Dr. Blotchmore's office," said Susan.

"Hi, this is Andrea Reed," said a girl's voice. "I had an appointment with the doctor this afternoon."

"At two," said Susan. "Are you calling to confirm?"

"Actually, no, I was calling to cancel."

After the briefest of pauses, Susan said, "I see. Would you like to reschedule, Andrea?"

Dr. Blotchmore tried to put a face with the name. Reed . . . Andrea Reed . . . . Was she that nervous girl with the wispy brown hair and glasses? Her acne had been pretty bad, as he'd remembered. She'd had a slight stammer, also.

But there wasn't a trace of a stammer in her voice now. "No, that's okay," she said. "My skin's fine."

"FINE?!" exclaimed Dr. Blotchmore, as if

she'd just delivered a personal insult.

"Dr. Blotchmore?" asked Andrea. "Is that you?"

"Yes, Andrea, it's me. And I'm a little concerned that you're canceling your appointment," he said. "In my opinion, it's premature. Very premature. As I recall, your skin needed extensive treatment."

"Not anymore," said Andrea. "It's all better. I'm healed," she added, sounding infuriatingly confident and happy.

The doctor struggled to keep his mounting feelings of outrage under control. "And how did that happen, may I ask?"

"Zit Boy," she answered. Before he had a chance to question her further, she said, "Whoops, gotta go, Dr. B. See ya!" and hung up.

"Zit Boy? Now I've heard everything," said Rufus Blotchmore. "Susan? Susan? Are you still there?"

"Yes, Doctor."

"Did any of the other cancellations reschedule?"

"No."

It took a moment for the implications of this to hit him. They were extremely bad. "Did any of them tell you why they were canceling?" he asked.

She thought for a moment. "Not at first. But when I asked them if they wanted to make another appointment, they all said the same thing."

"Really? What?" asked the doctor.

"They all said, 'I don't have to. I'm healed.'"

* 🔔 *

"Zit Boy? Is that really what he calls himself?" said Doona Scolder, shifting in her seat very slightly so she could see her face in the car's side mirror. The pimple was still there. *Persistent little thing,* she thought uneasily. *Doesn't seem to want to go away.*

I'd better watch my diet for a while.

On this sunny April afternoon she and Moldy were heading north on New York's Henry Hutchinson Parkway, bound for Westchester County. Reports had been coming out of Scarsdale about a teenage boy with mysterious powers, a charismatic figure called Chris Flartenberg by some, Zit Boy by others. Either way, both Moldy and Scolder were eager to meet him, for reasons they hadn't discussed with each other.

"No, that's what the kids started calling him—after he began to heal them," said Moldy. "It's a title of respect, according to The Secretives."

"Amazing."

"No more amazing than what he's supposed to be able to do," said Moldy, stealing a look at himself in the driver's side mirror. *Rats!* he thought. *The pimple's still there! Why won't it go away?*

"You say he claims to heal acne?" asked

Scolder, her hand moving of its own accord to the blemish on her face. She'd covered it with concealer, but she couldn't forget that it was there.

"With just a touch of his hand," said Moldy, with the special intensity that came into his voice whenever he discussed the paranormal. It was a subject dear to his heart, as Scolder knew very well.

"Witnesses have seen it happen, Scolder," he continued. "They say it's nothing short of miraculous." *What if it's true?* thought Moldy, feeling a thrill of hope. *What if Zit Boy could take care of my pimple?*

"Hmmm," said Scolder with a studied lack of emotion. She'd learned to respond to Moldy's ideas politely, though sometimes the price of her restraint was a fit of giggles over her bedtime cup of Ovaltine. More than once she'd snorted the hot liquid through her nose, which was extremely painful.

Now, however, she felt more than polite

interest. *What if it's true?* she thought, touching her face. *What if Zit Boy could take care of my pimple?*

"Gummi bear?" Moldy popped a handful of the gaily colored candies into his mouth and offered the bag to Scolder.

"No thanks," she said, waving it away.

"Have one, Scolder, they're good for you," Moldy joked.

"If only they were," she replied. "The truth is, Moldy, they have no nutritional value whatsoever, and you know it. Moreover, a recent study published in *Lancet*, the journal of British medicine, suggests that gummi candy may even be harmful—a possible cause of premature male pattern baldness."

"Baldness? Gummi candy?" Moldy choked a little bit as he swallowed the candy in his mouth. "Really? How? They're just sugar and food coloring." He glanced nervously at his partner.

She was grinning at him.

"Gotcha," said Scolder.

"Gotcha!" muttered Dr. Rufus Blotchmore to his computer screen. He'd finally found the Web site he'd been looking for all afternoon: www.zitboy.com. Now he knew why his teenage patients had been deserting him. Incredible as it seemed, they'd been seeing this…charlatan instead!

"'Zit Boy! The Teen Formerly Known as Flartenberg!'" read Blotchmore with a mixture of scorn and disbelief. "How can he be healing them? It's not possible!"

He scanned the site's list of entries:

MIRACLE BOY OR ZIT BOY? HIS FANS LOVE HIM EITHER WAY

HE CURED MORE THAN MY ZITS: A FORMER ADDICT TELLS HER STORY

"NO MORE SCARS IN SCARSDALE," VOWS YOUNG HEALER

The last entry caught Blotchmore's eye. He clicked on it and learned that Zit Boy was holding a meeting tonight at seven-thirty.

A malicious sneer spread over the doctor's face until he looked like a gargoyle in a bow tie. "Meet Zit Boy in person?" he exclaimed. "The sooner the better!"

He found the meeting without much trouble. After all, he knew the neighborhood—it was the wealthiest in Scarsdale. He even knew the address; it belonged to one of his former patients—a girl called Celia Barton.

Obnoxious girl, thought the doctor as he parked his Range Rover. Rude, vain, and rich—the only child of one of the most successful developers in Westchester. Their house was an enormous mock Tudor affair, complete with exposed cross beams and mullioned windows. The six-car garage even had a fake thatched roof. *They must have money to burn*, thought the doctor. *And some of that should still be coming to me!* added the angry inner voice that had been goading him on all day. *To me!*

A small sign on the immaculate lawn directed him to a footpath that took him along the south side of the house, and then to a brightly lit outbuilding. It must be a pool house, he thought, recognizing the smell of chlorine.

He stepped inside. It was as big as a football field.

About two dozen people, mostly teenagers, sat on folding chairs lined up to the right of the Olympic-sized pool. Celia Barton, looking cheerful and relaxed, made a few welcoming remarks. Her audience was so attentive, it might have been hypnotized; nobody even turned around when Blotchmore came in.

They'll be paying attention to me soon enough, said the angry voice inside his head. *Soon enough!*

He drew closer to the group.

Chris sensed something unusual about the gathering tonight, and understood why when he scanned the room. Adults! There were adults here! This was a first. Nobody but kids his age, mostly kids he recognized from school, had ever come to a meeting before. Who were these people? Strangers to him, though they fit right into the suburban setting. Both the man and the woman were well groomed, neat, and dressed in dark suits. They sat right in the front row, watching him intently. He wondered why they'd come. Their skin looked okay.

Then his attention shifted to Jennifer, who was getting ready to lead the first acne victim up to him. Their eyes met for an instant, and his heart jumped. She really loved him, and not just because he was Zit Boy, either. He knew that now. Even when it was all over—and that time was fast approaching—they'd be together.

"I'll still love you even when you're just Chris," Jennifer had promised.

He was kind of looking forward to it.

Special Agent Doona Scolder found that her skepticism about Zit Boy faded quickly once he appeared. A medium-tall, dark-haired boy with alert dark eyes, his face was open and likable. After greeting the audience quietly, he asked for the first acne sufferer. An unhappy-looking girl, heavily afflicted with both whiteheads and blackheads, was led up to him.

He took her face in his hands and closed his eyes. At that moment the only sound in the room was the slip-slap of water in the enormous pool. Nobody moved. Nobody breathed.

Zit Boy sighed and ran his fingertips back and forth, back and forth down the girl's face, almost as if he were reading Braille. They finally stopped, coming to rest almost abruptly at his sides. There were moans and exclamations from the audience. The girl's skin was clear. Zit Boy opened his eyes. He smiled at the girl, whose hands flew to her face, touching it where he had.

"Is it really gone?" she asked. He nodded, still smiling. The girl sobbed. Zit Boy patted her shoulder, looking so genuinely happy for her that tears welled up in Scolder's eyes. At that moment she heard a loud sniffle.

Moldy was crying. He turned to his partner. "Scolder . . ." he said brokenly, "I've got to talk to him! I've got this—"

"So do I," she interrupted, though her reply was lost in the loud applause and whoops of joy coming from the people around her. She stood. Moldy rose also, and they struggled together through the crowd until they were face-to-face with the young healer.

"Hi," he said, extending a welcoming hand to each of them. "I'm—"

Before he could continue, an angry shout, as jarring as a curse at a christening, came from the back of the room. With it, all the noisy celebration ended. Moldy and Scolder whirled around to see a balding, middle-aged man wearing a bow tie lurching toward the crowd.

"Stop, you fake!" he shouted at Zit Boy. "Stop stealing my patients, you good-for-nothing phony!"

"Oh, my God!!" exclaimed Celia Barton. "It's Blotchmore! And he's totally lost it!"

"Blotchmore? Dr. Blotchmore the dermatologist?" asked Zit Boy uncertainly.

Moldy and Scolder watched Blotchmore's jerky progress along the edge of the pool.

They saw him stumble, and they saw him reach into the breast pocket of his jacket. Was it their finely tuned reflexes responding with breathtaking speed to the sudden threat of violence? Or simply their profound annoyance at being interrupted before Zit Boy could heal their pimples? Whatever the reason, Moldy and Scolder's guns were drawn, and they were shouting, "Stop! FBI!" before Blotchmore's hand could move another inch.

There was a stunned silence. The doctor, visibly terrified at the sight of two very large handguns aimed straight at his heart, staggered backwards, lost his balance, and fell into the deep end of the pool.

He sank, bobbed to the surface, and screamed, "Help! I can't swim!" before he swallowed, choked, and went down again.

Scolder and Moldy were both good swimmers. But Scolder had just had her hair done, and Moldy was wearing an expensive new silk tie. They looked at each other, then at the group of teenagers who had gathered at the edge of the pool.

Nobody moved. It seemed the doctor was not a popular man.

"Damn," muttered Scolder, setting down her gun and stepping out of her heels. "*Rats!*" thought Moldy, shucking his jacket. Before either of them could jump in, Zit Boy stripped down to his shorts, dove quietly into the water, and surfaced next to the doctor. Calmly ducking Blotchmore's frantically windmilling arms, he towed him, still struggling, to the shallow end of the pool. There Blotchmore stood, coughing and sputtering, while Zit Boy vaulted out of the pool and into the arms of a blond girl who wrapped him in a towel and kissed him. They were quickly surrounded by the rest of the teens at the gathering.

Meanwhile, Moldy and Scolder seized Blotchmore's water pistol, escorted him out of the pool house, and listened impassively as he complained about his ungrateful patients on the way to his car.

"So what if the ointment was a little weak?" he said loudly. "So what if it took longer than the over-the-counter stuff? It worked—eventually!"

"Are you saying the medication you prescribed to your acne patients was less effective than standard drugstore brands?" Scolder asked, in a voice so neutral that even Moldy couldn't sense her disgust.

"Not less effective! Slower!"

"To someone with acne, slower is less effective," Moldy pointed out helpfully.

Blotchmore ignored him. "Impatience?" he hurried on. "Impatience? That's no reason to desert your dermatologist! Why are these kids in such a hurry, anyway? They have their whole lives ahead of them!"

He stopped at a gleaming new Range Rover with MD plates. The sight of it seemed to have a calming effect on him. "Here we are," he said, pulling his keys out of his damp coat pocket. "As for that Zit Boy character," he blustered, opening the car door, "he'd better watch out, because—"

"Because he can heal people without drugs?" said Scolder.

"Instantly? With just a touch of his hand?" asked Moldy.

"Because he's not doing it for material gain?" asked Scolder.

"But purely out of compassion?" added Moldy. The agents looked at the doctor, and suddenly the unpleasant word "malpractice" began to flash a warning in his agitated brain, almost as if they had conjured it up.

"All right, all right, enough! I see your point," said Blotchmore, dropping into the driver's seat. "By the way," he said, starting the car, "how about answering a question for me?"

They nodded.

"What are you, some kind of comedy act?"

He was gone before they could reply.

·　🪦　·

By the time Scolder and Moldy got back to the pool house, it was empty except for Zit Boy, the blond girl, and Celia Barton. They were deep in conversation, but fell silent as the agents approached.

"That was quite a rescue," Moldy said to the boy. "You saved his life."

"It was nothing," answered the boy, flushing.

"Chris is modest," said the blond girl. She took his hand.

"Thanks, Jennifer," said Chris.

"Are you guys really FBI agents, or what?" Celia asked. "Because we were wondering why you came."

"Chris wasn't doing anything illegal, was he?" Jennifer asked. "I mean, he was just trying to help. That's allowed, isn't it?"

"Besides," said Chris, "I'm stopping."

"Really?" exclaimed both agents at once.

"Yes. What happened tonight was too freaky. Too dangerous. I don't want to be responsible for some crime or terrible accident," said Chris. He looked at Jennifer, who smiled at him encouragingly. "I just want to be normal."

"Can I see you in private?" asked Moldy hastily.

"And then I wonder if I could have a word with you alone," said Scolder.

"Sure," said Chris. He'd done enough healing by now so that requests like this didn't surprise him anymore. He knew what they were about.

He rose. "Which one of you would like to go first?" he asked.

From the case notes of Doona Scolder:

My complexion is clear again,
much clearer than the strange
events surrounding our visit to
Scarsdale. Not only did Zit Boy
heal my pimple, he maintained
that his powers came, at least
in part, from Dr. Rufus
Blotchmore's ointment. We know
better. By the doctor's own
admission, the ointment was a
fake.

Which leads me to admit-
reluctantly-that my partner's
unwavering belief in the
existence of paranormal forces
may be valid, after all. What
is Zit Boy's power to heal if
not proof of such forces? I
witnessed a cure myself. And
though I have tried, I can

find no rational or scientific
explanation for it.

The truth is, Zit Boy worked
a small miracle.

Will I admit this to Moldy?
Doona Scolder smiled.

Not unless he tells me what
he asked Zit Boy in private.
Which thus far he has refused
to do.

Perhaps he will change his
mind one day. Until then, this
Hoax File is closed.

Get caught
in a web of danger!

www.SimonSaysKids.com
/net-scene

• • • • • • • • • •

If you love to surf—the net, that is—log on
for a suspense-filled ride through the web
with **danger.com**. Then click on to
www.SimonSaysKids.com/net-scene to

Win books!

Crack codes!

Chat with other fans!

Download cool stuff!

Meet the characters!

Boot up the danger.com web site—before
someone else beats you to it.

danger.com

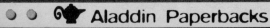

Aladdin Paperbacks